William Shakespeare's

The Taming of the Shrew

Tamara Hollingsworth
and Harriet Isecke, M.S.Ed.

Publishing Credits

Dona Herweck Rice, *Editor-in-Chief*; Lee Aucoin, *Creative Director*; Don Tran, *Print Production Manager;* Timothy J. Bradley, *Illustration Manager*; Wendy Conklin, M.A., *Senior Editor*; Torrey Maloof, *Associate Editor*; Lesley Palmer, *Cover Designer;* Rusty Kinnunen, *Illustrator;* Stephanie Reid, *Photo Editor*; Rachelle Cracchiolo, M.A. Ed., *Publisher*

Image Credits

cover & p.1 "The Gentle Katherine," *The Taming of the Shrew*, Act II Scene 1, illustration from *Tales from Shakespeare* by Charles and Mary Lamb, illustration by Norman Mills Price/Private Collection/The Stapleton Collection/The Bridgeman Art Library

Teacher Created Materials

5301 Oceanus Drive
Huntington Beach, CA 92649-1030
http://www.tcmpub.com
ISBN 978-1-4333-1276-2
©2010 Teacher Created Materials, Inc.
Printed in China

The Taming of the Shrew
Story Summary

In *The Taming of the Shrew*, a wealthy man named Baptista wants to marry off his daughters. His youngest daughter, Bianca, is beautiful, demure, and eager to become someone's wife. His older daughter, Kate, is beautiful, but she is ill-tempered and defiant. Baptista makes a rule that before Bianca can marry, Kate must marry. Bianca's suitors set to work finding a brave man to marry Kate.

Tips for Performing Reader's Theater

Adapted from Aaron Shepard

- Do not let your script hide your face. If you cannot see the audience, your script is too high.

- Look up often when you speak. Do not just look at your script.

- Speak slowly so the audience knows what you are saying.

- Speak loudly so everyone can hear you.

- Speak with feeling. If the character is sad, let your voice be sad. If the character is surprised, let your voice be surprised.

- Stand up straight. Keep your hands and feet still.

- Remember that even when you are not speaking, you are still your character.

Tips for Performing
Reader's Theater *(cont.)*

- If the audience laughs, wait for the laughter to stop before you speak again.

- If someone in the audience talks, do not pay attention.

- If someone walks into the room, do not pay attention.

- If you make a mistake, pretend it was right.

- If you drop something, try to leave it where it is until the audience is looking somewhere else.

- If a reader forgets to read his or her part, see if you can read the part instead, make something up, or just skip over it. Do not whisper to the reader!

The Taming
of the Shrew

Characters

Baptista	Hortensio
Kate	Bianca
Lucentio	Petruchio

Setting

This reader's theater is set in the Italian city of Padua. Much of the action takes place in and around the homes of Baptista and Hortensio. There are also scenes at the country house of Petruchio.

Act I, Scene I

At the home of Baptista

Baptista: Good day, gentlemen of Padua. I know that you both came to pursue my daughter, Bianca. However, my youngest may not marry until I have a husband for my eldest. If either of you would like to court Kate, I freely give you permission to do so.

Hortensio: *Cart* her, maybe, but not court her. She is far too much for me.

Kate: May I ask, Father, is it your intention to humiliate me publicly? Why are you showing me off like a horse in front of these absurd suitors?

Hortensio: We are not your suitors, for sure, unless you improve your awful temper. Lord, please keep me safe from women like her.

Kate: Do you have something you wish to say directly to me?

Bianca: Please, Kate. Do not be rude.

Kate: No man will make nasty insinuations about me without the courage to do so to my face. I have no interest in you. Although, I would not mind hitting you hard in the head with a three-legged stool, painting your face with blood, and making a fool out of you!

Lucentio: I am sure that Hortensio meant no great harm, Kate. It is just that your sister is quiet and well behaved, as a lady should be. In contrast, although my eyes see that you are lovely, you do not always act in a very friendly manner, pretty Kate.

Kate: What have you to do with this, and what right do you think you have to call me *pretty*? You are pathetic if you think you can quickly melt the heart of a woman with a simple compliment.

Bianca: Please, Kate, calm down. Father, I fear Kate will never marry, so neither will I. I will comfort myself with my books and instruments. They will be my only company.

Baptista: Bianca, go inside and do not dwell on your unhappiness. I assure you, I will love you the same, whether you are married or not.

Bianca: I will go, Father, and try to find happiness in my great unhappiness.

Kate: She would make herself cry pitifully if she only knew how.

Hortensio: I am sorry that our affections for Bianca are causing her such grief. Baptista, can you really be this cruel?

Baptista: I am resolved on this decision. Now, because Bianca takes delight in music and poetry, I want to hire tutors for her and Kate. If you know any suitable tutors, please send them to me. Gentlemen and Kate, you may stay here. I must leave, for I have things to discuss with Bianca.

Kate: Stay here? Ha! I will not be told where to stay and where to go like a child. I am leaving, now!

Hortensio: Go where you please. You have nothing that we want. Oh, Lucentio, it seems to be a lost cause. What will we do now?

Lucentio: I am smitten with Bianca. I saw her coral lips move and the air was perfumed with her very breath. It will be a happy man who claims Bianca, and if we both still want to vie for that chance, we must work together.

Hortensio: What do you mean?

Lucentio: We need to find a suitor for Kate.

Hortensio: That is impossible! No man will ever marry a vicious woman like Kate. She is a shrew with a cruel tongue and a sharp wit.

Lucentio: I do not know. But we must find someone!

Hortensio: Kate will never submit to a husband. What man would relish such a wife?

Lucentio: But neither of us will be able to woo the glorious and delicate Bianca until Kate is wed. We must think of something!

Hortensio: Wait! I know! My good friend, Petruchio, is coming into town from Verona. In fact, he is coming this very evening. I will speak with him about this matter.

Lucentio: Do you think he would be interested in Kate?

Hortensio: If Baptista offers a large enough dowry, he may be. Although, as his friend, I must warn Petruchio. I must tell him of Kate's harsh temper.

Act I, Scene II

Hortensio's house

Hortensio: Hello, Petruchio. You do not look well. What brings you to Padua?

Petruchio: My situation looks bleak, Hortensio. My father is dead, and so I have set off to see if I can marry well. I have been traveling around, having fantastic adventures, but I have run out of traveling money. So I come to Padua with the intent to find a wealthy wife.

Hortensio: I know where you can find a shrewish and unpleasant wife. I doubt you would thank me, but she is very rich.

Petruchio: Well, money is exactly what I am looking for! I could care less if a woman is old, ugly, or bad tempered. The one quality I am looking for in the woman I marry is great fortune.

Hortensio: The young lady I mention is beautiful. There is no doubt of that. But, as I have warned you, her temper does not match her beauty.

Petruchio: Well, as long as her wealth matches her beauty and not her temperament, then I am interested!

Hortensio: That, my friend, is the good news for you. Her father will offer a sizable dowry to any man who will marry her. He has had many problems with suitors. The young lady refuses them all.

Petruchio: Let me go tomorrow, and I will speak with her father.

Hortensio: I must be completely honest, my friend. She is so disagreeable that in the city they have a special name for her. They call her Kate the Cursed.

Petruchio: A woman with fire raging in her! I am intrigued. Do not worry, Hortensio. I have fought lions in the jungles and heard the mighty sea roar in anger at me. There is no woman, no matter how impassioned with hatred, who can scare me.

Hortensio: You better get your rest now, Petruchio. You will surely need your full strength tomorrow.

Petruchio: Good night, my friend. I look forward to the morn.

Hortensio: Good night, Petruchio.

Act I, Scene III

Hortensio's house

Hortensio: Is that knocking at the door I hear? I wonder who could be calling at such a late hour. Who is it?

Lucentio: It is me, Lucentio. I was wondering how the plan we spoke about is coming together?

Hortensio: Ah, hello, Lucentio. The plan is going well. In fact, even though I warned Petruchio about Kate, he was delighted with the idea. He does not care what she is like as long as she will bring him a fortune.

Lucentio: That is great news, Hortensio! Now, I have something else I wanted to let you know. I have devised a way to meet with Bianca. You heard Baptista request tutors for his daughters. I will call myself Cambio and dress as a tutor. I will use our lessons as a time to express my love to Bianca.

Hortensio: What shall I do to have access to the beautiful Bianca?

Lucentio: Maybe you can dress up as a music tutor.

Hortensio: That is a great idea! I will do it! I think I shall call myself Litio. I will tell Petruchio.

Act II, Scene I

The home of Baptista

Bianca: Kate, please do not make a slave of me by refusing to marry. I know that you do not want to be married, but it is the wisest choice for a woman.

Kate: Bianca, who among your suitors is your true love?

Bianca: I do not know that I love any of them. There is no special face, as yet, that I prefer to all others.

Kate: I bet you are hoping that a suitor will provide you with great fortune, Bianca. I think that is why you are so terribly distraught about not marrying.

Bianca: Do not be so cruel, Kate. Stop trying to make me weep. I just want a husband to belong to.

Kate: Well, I will belong to no man.

Bianca: You belong to Father.

Kate: You are ridiculous, Bianca. How cruel and absurd it is to be a woman. Why should the world define us by the men who own us?

Bianca: You are impossible, Kate!

Baptista: What is that pitiful crying that I am hearing? What did you do, Kate, to make your poor sister so hysterical? Why do you treat her like a fiend?

Kate: You do not want to hear my side, do you, Father? Of course not, for Bianca is your precious little treasure who must have a husband, and I must dance barefoot on her wedding day.

Baptista: Go upstairs and get out of my sight, Kate. Ah, I see more suitors. Good morning, gentlemen. I am tired this morning and must tell you that I will speak with no man about Bianca.

Petruchio: Well then, good sir, we shall speak more then, since I do not come to speak about Bianca. I have come to ask you about marrying your first daughter, Kate. My name is Petruchio, a man well known throughout Italy.

Baptista: Kate, you say? And who are these friends with you?

Lucentio: My name is Cambio. I have come to offer my services as a Greek and Latin teacher to your daughters.

Hortensio: I am Litio. I have come to give your daughters music lessons.

Baptista: Good then, young men, you may go to your pupils. They are upstairs. Petruchio, let us discuss your desire to marry Kate. I was wondering how you know of her.

Petruchio: Although I have never met her, I heard of your lovely daughter and of her virtue, beauty, grace, and quiet elegance. I came from Verona to ask for her hand in marriage.

Baptista: Let us walk through the orchard and talk about this further.

Act II, Scene II

Baptista's orchard

Petruchio: Sir, I am sorry to be in such a rush, but I have been on a journey away from home for a long time and desire a hasty return. So, assuming that I win your daughter's love, what kind of dowry would you offer for her?

Baptista: I offer twenty thousand crowns now, and I offer half my lands when I leave this world. But first, you must convince Kate to marry you, and that will be a very difficult task.

Petruchio: Do not worry. I can be exceptionally stubborn. I am as commanding as she is proud minded. When two raging fires meet, they consume the thing that feeds their fury. I can easily match her passion, and with my own, subdue hers.

Baptista: Well, good luck then, but be prepared for some unhappy words.

Petruchio: Sir, I am most prepared. Mountains do not tremble even when a strong wind is blowing.

Act II, Scene III

Baptista's house

Baptista: What has happened to you, Litio? Why are you so pale?

Hortensio: My head is cut and bleeding. I am pale from fear.

Baptista: Will my daughters prove to be good musicians?

Hortensio: Your daughter, Kate, would sooner prove to be a soldier! She may be good with firearms, but never with lutes.

Baptista: Are you saying you cannot break her into playing the lute?

Hortensio: I am saying that she broke the lute on me. When I tried to show her the proper fingering, she jumped and yelled, "Frets, call you these?" and hit me on the head with the lute.

Petruchio: This lusty creature has real character! I love her ten times more than I did before and cannot wait to meet her.

Baptista: Do not get discouraged, Litio. Just continue the lessons with my younger daughter, Bianca. She will be most pleasant and learn quickly. And, Petruchio, wait here. I will send my older daughter to you. Good luck!

Petruchio: How shall I woo such a woman? I will take a novel approach and do it with spirit. I will pretend her words mean the opposite of what they actually do. When she screeches and rants, I will claim she sings like a beautiful nightingale. If she is coldly silent, I will praise her chattiness. Ah, here she comes now. Hello, Kate. I hear that is your name.

Kate: You must be hard of hearing. I am Katherine.

Petruchio: No, you lie, you are called Kate. Sometimes you are called plain Kate, or bonny Kate, or Kate the Cursed, or Kate the Shrew, but I will call you the prettiest Kate in the world. Hearing of you, Kate, I was moved to come here to marry you.

Kate: Well, just move yourself somewhere else then. I am not interested.

Petruchio: Come, Kate! Do not be angry like a wasp.

Kate: If I be waspish, you best beware my sting.

Petruchio: It cannot hurt me, for as all men know, the stinger is in the tail of a wasp and can be easily removed.

Kate: Yes, but mine lies in my tongue, where you cannot get it.

Petruchio: No sting of yours is great enough to damage me, good Kate. I see that the others have been all wrong about you, for you are funny, playful, and beautifully behaved. We will marry on Sunday.

Kate: I would rather see you hanged on Sunday.

Petruchio: I will see your arms hanging around my neck as you kiss me on Sunday.

Baptista: How is everything going? Are you two getting along?

Petruchio: Getting along? We are to be married this Sunday!

Baptista: Sunday? Married? How wonderful. What a match!

Poem: Sonnet 70

Act III, Scene 1

The wedding

Baptista: It seems that the entire town has shown up at church to see if Petruchio will actually marry you, Kate. He is very late, and I worry that he has changed his mind.

Kate: I complained that Petruchio was an absolute madman, Father. He has no intention of coming. He probably leaves women standing at the altar all the time. Now the whole world will make fun of me. I am humiliated!

Bianca: Father, I see Petruchio coming. But I worry for my sister. He is dressed like a pirate, with red and blue garters, a stocking on one leg and a woolen booty on the other. He actually looks quite insane.

Baptista: I am just glad he is coming!

Petruchio: Where is my bride? Where is the beautiful Kate?

Bianca: This is how you dress for your wedding to my sister?

Baptista: Why do you look like that? Are you drunk? Surely you do not plan to marry Kate in those clothes.

Petruchio: Of course I will. Kate comes to marry me and not my clothes.

Act III, Scene II

The wedding reception

Hortensio: I have never seen a wedding like this.

Lucentio: Neither have I. Kate is a peaceful dove compared to Petruchio. When the priest asked Kate if she would have him, Petruchio answered for her and swore so loudly that the priest dropped the prayer book. Listen, I hear them fighting already!

Petruchio: Thank you all for coming to our wedding celebration. Unfortunately, Kate and I cannot feast. We must leave immediately.

Kate: Please, let me plead with you to stay in Padua.

Petruchio: I am content.

Kate: To stay here?

Petruchio: No, I am content to let you plead with me. But we leave tonight.

Kate: Do whatever you want, Petruchio, but I will not leave until I am good and ready. I can only imagine how arrogant you will be as a husband. Now everyone, it is time for the bridal dinner.

Petruchio: The guests shall go to the dinner at your command, Kate, but you are coming with me.

Bianca: What? You will not let my sister attend her own bridal dinner? For what reason?

Petruchio: I am master of my possessions, and Kate is my possession, just like my house, my field, and my horses.

Bianca: Can't she just stay for a little while?

Petruchio: No, we are leaving right now. Come, Kate!

Baptista: Now guests, though the bride and groom will not take places at the table, there is no food missing at this feast. Let us go and rejoice!

Lucentio: Baptista, may I sit next to your beautiful daughter, Bianca? I have something I want to read to her in Latin.

Baptista: Certainly you may, Cambio. She seems quite taken with your teaching. There she is now.

Lucentio: Bianca, now that your sister is married, I want to declare my eternal love to you in this Latin poem. I confess that I am really not the poor teacher, Cambio, who I have pretended to be.

Bianca: What do you mean? Who are you?

Lucentio: I hope you can forgive me. I disguised myself to have a chance to be near you. I am Lucentio. Do you think you could love me, sweet Bianca?

Bianca: Yes, Lucentio, I forgive you and love you!

Lucentio: Then I will speak to your father.

Act IV, Scene I

Petruchio's country house

Kate: I am exhausted and starving after traveling all night. I see the servants are bringing some warm and delicious-looking food.

Petruchio: What is this slop? How dare you bring us such food?

Kate: This food is good and warm, and it tastes fine, Petruchio.

Petruchio: Servants, take this sickening glop away at once. Never will such disgusting food touch your precious lips, Kate.

Kate: But there is nothing wrong with the food, and I am famished from the long and tedious journey here.

Petruchio: No, servants, take it away at once. My Kate, you are too wonderful to eat such trash.

Kate: I am going to bed then. Good night.

Petruchio: I will kill my wife with kindness, and thereby curb her headstrong ways. Servants, go up every hour to change my wife's sheets and pillows. Keep her up all night.

Act IV, Scene II

A few days later at Petruchio's country house

Petruchio: Kate, you seem exhausted. I wish I had food good enough to serve you and a bed clean enough for you to sleep in.

Kate: Petruchio, maybe you need to be a bit more patient. I need food and sleep more than perfection.

Petruchio: It is absolutely unthinkable, Kate! I will not stand for you to have any less than you deserve. Wait, I hear knocking and must see who is there. My friend Hortensio, what brings you this long distance?

Hortensio: I have much news to tell. Bianca has declared her love for Lucentio, and not me. I will marry a wealthy widow, instead. Petruchio, you and Kate are invited to Bianca's wedding tomorrow. I must return now. I will see you at the celebration.

Petruchio: I will have the finest dress made for you, Kate. I will send a message to the tailor immediately.

Act IV, Scene III

Later that day at Petruchio's country house

Kate: This fabric is beautiful, tailor. I would like the dress to be special for my sister's wedding.

Petruchio: All of the fabric you show us looks cheap. What other choices are there? You will have only the best, my beloved Kate.

Kate: There are no other choices, Husband.

Petruchio: If there are no other choices, then you will go without a dress. I will not have my wife, my glorious Kate, dressed in simple and rough fabrics.

Kate: I know what you are doing. You are denying me food and clothing and the basic needs all in the name of love. This foolishness must stop.

Petruchio: Truly, Kate, you may only have the finest things, for I will allow nothing inferior. Away now, tailor, and take your cheap fabrics.

Act IV, Scene IV

The next day on the road to Padua

Kate: We should have left earlier, Petruchio. I am afraid we will not make it by evening. The travel is rough, and the sun is so bright.

Petruchio: You constantly contradict me, Kate. I tell you it is 7:00 AM and you tell me it is 2:00 PM. What you see is the moon, not the sun, my lovely Kate.

Kate: First, you tell me that old man we passed was a woman, and now you tell me the moon is the sun. It is the afternoon and the moon shines only at night.

Petruchio: Maybe this trip is too difficult and we should not go at all. If you cannot tell the moon from the sun, maybe we should not go any farther today.

Kate: Yes, fine. I am so very weary. It is the moon, and if you want to call it a candle from now on, so it will be.

Petruchio: Come now and kiss me, Kate! You look more beautiful now than you ever have before.

Song: Sonnet 138

Act V, Scene I

Bianca's wedding reception

Baptista: I rejoice that I have two daughters, both married. I have much pity for you, Petruchio. I can only guess what you must deal with in terms of Kate.

Lucentio: Yes, I feel lucky to have the beautiful and submissive Bianca. You must struggle a great deal with Kate.

Petruchio: No, my good gentlemen, you misunderstand Kate. She is a wonderful wife.

Baptista: She lived in my house many years, and I would not describe her behavior as wonderful.

Petruchio: Let's see then. I will bet you that if we call for our wives, Kate will come to me without hesitation.

Lucentio: This I must see. Kate is a shrew. Bianca will come before Kate will.

Petruchio: Let us make a wager of 20 crowns. Servants, tell our wives to come to us. Give the women no other reason than that we want them to come immediately.

Lucentio: You look confident that she will come. I would not be so sure, if I were you.

Petruchio: She will come. I have no fear. Look, though I see no sign of Bianca, Kate flies to me now.

Kate: What is it that you wish, Husband?

Petruchio: Only to see you, my love. You have been from my sight for too long.

Kate: Do not be silly, Petruchio. Oh, Lucentio, my sister says she is busy and cannot come to you right now. I was enjoying my sister's company, Petruchio, but I will stay here if you wish.

Petruchio: No, it is not necessary, my wife. Go and be with your sister, but first, kiss me, Kate.

Kate: Gladly, Husband. Whatever you say, I will do.

Baptista: Petruchio, it is a miracle. You have tamed a terrible shrew.

Lucentio: The true miracle is that she let herself be tamed.

Sonnet 70
William Shakespeare

That thou art blamed shall not be thy defect,

For slander's mark was ever yet the fair;

The ornament of beauty is suspect,

A crow that flies in heaven's sweetest air.

So thou be good, slander doth but approve

Thy worth the greater, being wooed of time,

For canker vice the sweetest buds doth love,

And thou present'st a pure unstained prime.

Thou hast passed by the ambush of young days,

Either not assail'd, or victor being charged,

Yet this thy praise cannot be so thy praise

To tie up envy, evermore enlarged:

    If some suspect of ill maskt not thy show,

    Then thou alone kingdoms of hearts shouldst owe.

Sonnet 138

William Shakespeare

When my love swears that she is made of truth,
I do believe her, though I know she lies,
That she might think me some untutor'd youth,
Unlearned in the world's false subtleties.
Thus vainly thinking that she thinks me young,
Although she knows my days are past the best,
Simply I credit her false-speaking tongue;
On both sides thus is simple truth supprest.
But wherefore says she not she is unjust?
And wherefore say not I that I am old?
O love's best habit is in seeming trust,
And age in love loves not to have years told.
    Therefore I lie with her, and she with me,
    And in our faults by lies we flatter'd be.

Glossary

ambush—a surprise attack

canker—a plant disease marked by dead tissue

cart—to carry in, or as if in, a cart

court—to engage in a social relationship, usually leading to marriage

defect—a lack of something necessary for completeness or perfection

dowry—the property that a woman brings to her husband in marriage

humiliate—to cause a loss of pride or self-respect

insinuations—suggestions made in an indirect way

lute—a musical instrument resembling a guitar with a pear-shaped body

ornament—something that adds beauty

shrew—a scolding or bad-tempered woman

slander—the making of false statements that damage another's reputation

submissive—inclined or willing to submit to others

subtleties—qualities of being sly or crafty

suitors—men who court women or seek to marry them

temperament—a person's attitude as it affects what he or she says or does